The First Day of Winter

For Will, Jane, and Ian

SQUARE
FISH

An Imprint of Macmillan

THE FIRST DAY OF WINTER.
Copyright © 2005 by Denise Fleming.
All rights reserved. Printed in China by South China
Printing Company Ltd., Dongguan City,
Guangdong Province. For information, address
Square Fish, 175 Fifth Avenue, New York, NY 10010.

Square Fish and the Square Fish logo are trademarks
of Macmillan and are used by Henry Holt and Company
under license from Macmillan.

Library of Congress Cataloging-in-Publication Data
Fleming, Denise.
The first day of winter / Denise Fleming.
Summary: A snowman comes alive as the child building
it adds pieces during the first ten days of winter.
ISBN 978-0-312-37138-8
[1. Snowmen—Fiction. 2. Counting. 3. Stories in rhyme.]
I. Title.
PZ8.3.F6378Fi 2005
[E]—dc22   2004022181

Originally published in the United States by Henry Holt and Company
First Square Fish Edition: October 2012
Square Fish logo designed by Filomena Tuosto
mackids.com
F&P: I

4   6   8   10   9   7   5   3

The illustrations were created using colored cotton fiber, hand-cut stencils, and squeeze bottles.
Book design by Denise Fleming and David Powers. Visit denisefleming.com.

The First Day of Winter

Denise Fleming

SQUARE
FISH

Henry Holt and Company • New York

December

Sunday	Monday	Tuesday	Wednesday	Thursday	Friday	Saturday
		1	2	3	4	5
	7	8 ○	9	10	11	
14	15	16	17	◑	23	18
21	22			23	●	24
29					30	
8 ◑						

First Day of Winter

Christmas Eve

On the **first** day of winter

my best friend gave to me...

...a red cap with a gold snap.

On the **second** day of winter
my best friend gave to me
2 bright blue mittens
and a red cap with a gold snap.

On the **third** day of winter
my best friend gave to me
3 striped scarves,
2 bright blue mittens,
and a red cap with a gold snap.

On the **fourth** day of winter
my best friend gave to me
4 prickly pinecones,
3 striped scarves,
2 bright blue mittens,
and a red cap
with a gold snap.

On the **fifth** day of winter

my best friend gave to me

5 birdseed pockets,

4 prickly pinecones,

3 striped scarves,

2 bright blue mittens,

and a red cap with a gold snap.

On the sixth day of winter
my best friend gave to me
6 tiny twigs,
5 birdseed pockets,
4 prickly pinecones,
3 striped scarves,
2 bright blue mittens,
and a red cap
with a gold snap.

On the **seventh** day of winter
my best friend gave to me
7 maple leaves,
6 tiny twigs,
5 birdseed pockets,
4 prickly pinecones,
3 striped scarves,
2 bright blue mittens,
and a red cap with a gold snap.

On the **eighth** day of winter
my best friend gave to me
8 orange berries,
7 maple leaves,
6 tiny twigs,
5 birdseed pockets,
4 prickly pinecones,
3 striped scarves,
2 bright blue mittens,
and a red cap with a gold snap.

On the **ninth** day of winter
my best friend gave to me
9 big black buttons,
8 orange berries,
7 maple leaves,
6 tiny twigs,
5 birdseed pockets,
4 prickly pinecones,
3 striped scarves,
2 bright blue mittens,
and a red cap
with a gold snap.

On the **tenth** day of winter
my best friend gave to me
10 salty peanuts,
9 big black buttons,
8 orange berries,
7 maple leaves,
6 tiny twigs,
5 birdseed pockets,
4 prickly pinecones,
3 striped scarves,
2 bright blue mittens,
and a red cap
with a gold snap!